Finding a Job for Daddy

Evelyn Hughes Maslac

Illustrated by
Kay Life

Albert Whitman & Company • Morton Grove, Illinois

For Alan—here's the silver lining, sweetheart, with my love. Many thanks as well to Lily, Midge, and Cristy for all their help and encouragement. EHM

With love to the Lifes on Mountain Road. KL

Library of Congress Cataloging-in-Publication Data

Maslac, Evelyn Hughes.
    Finding a job for Daddy / written by Evelyn Hughes Maslac; illustrated by Kay Life.
        p.   cm.
    Summary: A young girl helps her father look for a new job and lets him know that he will always have the important job of being her daddy.
    ISBN 0-8075-2437-9
    [1. Fathers and daughters—Fiction. 2. Fathers—Employment—Fiction. 3. Job hunting—Fiction.]
I. Life, Kay, ill. II. Title.
PZ7.M376Fi 1996   95-36718
[E]—dc20   CIP
                                                      AC

The text of this book is set in Futura Book.
The illustrations are rendered in watercolor.
Design by Lucy Smith.

Laura ran through the schoolyard to Daddy. He was wearing his lucky tie—Laura's favorite. He always wore it to meet people who might give him a job.

"Daddy, you had an interview!" Laura said. "How was it?"

Daddy lifted Laura high in the air. "Well, I think they liked me, punkin."

NEW SUNDAY HOURS
STORE HOURS MONDAY THRU SATURDAY 8 AM TO 10 PM

"Are they going to give you a job?" Laura asked.

"I won't know for a while. They need time to think about it." Daddy took Laura's hand to cross the street. "Let's stop by the market. We need spaghetti."

"Can't we go out for dinner tonight?" said Laura.

Daddy shook his head. "No money for that right now, punkin."

"You could get some at the cash machine," Laura said.

"That only works if your money's in the bank to begin with," Daddy answered.

"But, Daddy, we never go—"

"Laura, that's enough!" Daddy said sharply. Then he sighed. "I'm sorry, honey, but until I find another job, there are lots of things we just can't afford to do anymore." He ruffled Laura's hair. "Will you help me with the want ads later?"

"Can I color them?" Laura asked.

Daddy smiled. "Your crayons are ready and waiting."

After dinner, Mommy did the dishes and Daddy and Laura sat down with the newspaper. Daddy opened the part where people advertised the jobs they wanted somebody to do.

"Here's one, Laura," Daddy said. He showed her a little box with some writing in it. "Can you make a big circle around it?" Laura did. Daddy turned the page. "And maybe that one, too," he said, showing her.

"Not much in there today?" Mommy asked.

"Only two," Daddy told her. "I'll get my résumé ready to mail after I read to Laura."

Laura followed Daddy to the living room. "What's a résumé?" she asked.

"It's a list of the good things you did on the jobs you had before," Daddy explained. "When you see an ad for a job you want, you send your résumé. If the people like it, then they call you."

Laura understood. "And you get an interview—with your lucky tie!"

Daddy nodded. "Right. That's when you go to their office. They ask you questions about what you've done, and you decide if you'd like working for them."

"Then they give you a job," Laura said.

"Sometimes," Daddy said. "Sometimes not."

"A lot of folks are looking for work right now," Mommy said from the kitchen.

"When you get a job, who'll take care of me after school?" Laura asked.

"A babysitter, like before," Daddy said. "We'll get someone you like."

"But I like *you*."

"Oh, punkin." Daddy pulled Laura onto his lap. "It's fun being with you. But I like to work, too, and we need the money I earn." He held Laura tightly. "I'll find something soon."

Before it got dark, Laura went outside to help Mommy in the garden. "Daddy was grouchy in the store today. I only said I wanted to go someplace for dinner."

"Being out of a job is hard on him," Mommy said.

Laura yanked out a weed. "He should've stayed at his old work."

"I wish he could have, but his work ran out of money to pay him."

"Will they ever give Daddy his job back?" Laura asked.

"I don't think so, sweetheart," Mommy said.

Laura looked up. "What if *your* work runs out of money? What if you lose *your* job?"

"I won't, honey. Everything's fine at my job." Mommy gave Laura a hug. "And don't worry about Daddy. He'll be a whole lot happier when he knows someone wants him for a job."

Laura lay in bed that night thinking about Daddy. She could hear him and Mommy talking in the living room. They used to giggle and act silly together sometimes, but not these days.

Their voices got louder. Laura pulled the blanket over her head.

The next morning, Laura woke up with an
idea. When she got to school, she went to work
on a surprise for Daddy. Her teacher helped with
the words, but Laura colored it all by herself.

At home, she waited until Daddy wasn't looking
and hid the first part of his surprise in the newspaper.
But Daddy didn't open the newspaper that afternoon.

He didn't open it while he was making dinner.
He didn't open it while Laura was setting the table.

By the time Mommy and Daddy had finished the dishes, Laura couldn't wait any longer.

"Daddy," she burst out, "we didn't color the want ads today!"

Daddy turned to her. "I read them earlier, punkin. There wasn't anything new."

"Yes, there is!" Laura protested. "I mean—you could've missed something! You should check again. Here!"

Mommy and Daddy looked at each other. "Okay," said Daddy. "I'll check." He took the newspaper. "Well, how about that," he said. "There *is* something new."

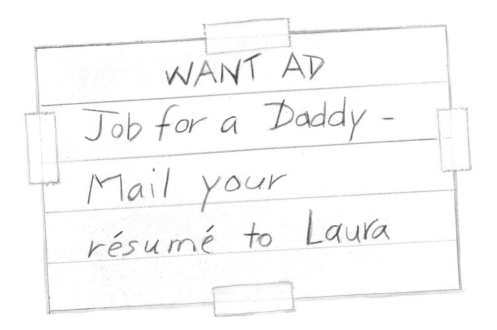

WANT AD

Job for a Daddy –

Mail your

résumé to Laura

"Well," said Mommy. "That certainly sounds like a good job."

"You're right," Daddy said. "I'll get my résumé."

"But Daddy, you won't need it," Laura said. "Look!" She handed him the second part of his surprise.

Daddy read it out loud.

My Daddy's Résumé
of Good Things for a Job

by Laura

1. He takes good care of me.

2. He puts sunburn stuff on my back. He lets me wear my teddy bear shoes with no socks if I want.

3. He gets me from school. We play horse, and we cook.

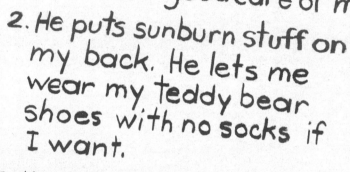

4. He gives me his baseball cap to wear to bed. He reads Charlotte's Web. He leaves the night-light on when it's too scary.

5. I love him.

"That's a wonderful résumé, Laura," Daddy said. "If I mail it, do you think I might get this job?"

Laura nodded. Daddy addressed an envelope. "I'll be the mail carrier," Mommy said. She took the envelope and turned to Laura. "Excuse me, miss. Is your name Laura?"

"Yes," said Laura.

"I have a letter for you. Will you accept delivery?" Mommy said.

"Yes, I will," said Laura. Mommy gave her Daddy's envelope.

Laura opened it and looked at the paper inside. "Good. Now I want an interview. You have to come to my office."

"You'd better put your tie on, dear," Mommy told Daddy.

Daddy put on his lucky tie and went to Laura's room. "Miss Laura?" he said. "I'm here for my interview."

Laura sat up very straight. "Do you want to be my daddy?"

"Yes, miss," said Daddy. "I do."

"And will you always do these good things?" Laura held up the résumé.

"Always, punkin." Daddy cleared his throat. "I mean, Miss Laura."

"Okay." Laura grinned at him. "You've got the job."

"I do?" Laughing, Daddy scooped Laura up
and kissed her. "This tie really *is* lucky!"

Laura beamed. "I know you still have to find
another job, Daddy," she said. "But you can have
this one forever!"